George Slythe Street

The Autobiography of a Boy

Passages Selected by His Friend

George Slythe Street

The Autobiography of a Boy
Passages Selected by His Friend

ISBN/EAN: 9783337015114

Printed in Europe, USA, Canada, Australia, Japan

Cover: Foto ©Raphael Reischuk / pixelio.de

More available books at **www.hansebooks.com**

THE MAYFAIR SET
I
THE
AUTOBIOGRAPHY
OF A BOY

THE MAYFAIR SET

Foolscap 8vo.   3s. 6d. each.

1. *The Autobiography of a Boy*, by G. S. STREET, *with Title-page designed by* C. W. FURSE.

2. *The Joneses and the Asterisks, a Story in Monologue*, by GERALD CAMPBELL, *with six Illustrations and a Title-page by* F. H. TOWNSEND.

3. *Select Conversations with an Uncle* (*now extinct*), by H. G. WELLS, *with a Title-page by* F. H. TOWNSEND.

(IN PREPARATION)

4. *For Plain Women only*, by GEORGE FLEMING.

5. *Mrs. Albert Grundy, Observations in Philistia*, by HAROLD FREDERIC.

6. *The Feasts of Autolycus, the Diary of a Greedy Woman, edited by* ELIZABETH ROBINS PENNELL.

THE AUTOBIOGRAPHY OF A BOY

PASSAGES
SELECTED
BY HIS FRIEND

G·S·STREET·

LONDON:
JOHN LANE·
NEW YORK:
THE MERRIAM
COMPANY·
·1895·

Fifth Edition

Edinburgh : T. and A. CONSTABLE, Printers to Her Majesty

THE EDITOR'S APOLOGY

In fulfilling a promise made to my friend, whom by your leave I will call simply Tubby, I have been conscious of a somewhat difficult dilemma. When he went to Canada, he placed the manuscript of his autobiography in my hands, with power to select and abridge. I perceived that if I published it in all its length nobody would read it : his life in England was not various, his orbit was circumscribed, the people he met and the situations he faced had a certain sameness, the comments he made on them dealt in repetitions. On the other hand, having made my selections on the principle of giving you none but typical incidents, and these but once, I find the result is meagre, and fear you may be angry at being troubled with it at all. Tubby himself was for publishing the whole. But craving your pardon, if you be angry, I think it is better to be amused (if amused you be) for an hour or so than to be bored for a day. I do assure you, you could have borne no more.

The autobiography covers only the period from his leaving Oxford to the other day, and it may therefore be well to give you a few facts of his earlier life, and perhaps a word or two concerning the period mentioned above, since I may be deceived by my intimate acquaintance with him in thinking that his mode of life, his point of view, and his peculiar qualities are indicated sufficiently by himself.

He was expelled from two private and one public school; but his private tutor gave him an excellent character, proving that the rough and ready methods of school-masters' appreciation were unsuited to the fineness of his nature. As a young boy he was not remarkable for distinction of the ordinary sort—at his prescribed studies and at games involving muscular strength and activity. But in very early life the infinite indulgence of his smile was famous, and as in after years was often misunderstood; it was even thought by his schoolfellows that its effect at a crisis in his career was largely responsible for the rigour with which he was treated by the authorities : ' they were not men of the world,' was the harshest comment he himself was ever known to make on them. He spoke with invariable kindness also of the dons at Oxford (who sent him down in his third year), com-plaining only that they had not absorbed the true atmosphere of the place, which he

loved. He was thought eccentric there, and
was well known only in a small and very
exclusive set. But a certain amount of
general popularity was secured to him by
the disfavour of the powers, his reputation
for wickedness, and the supposed magni-
ficence of his debts. His theory of life
also compelled him to be sometimes drunk.
In his first year he was a severe ritualist, in
his second an anarchist and an atheist, in
his third wearily indifferent to all things, in
which attitude he remained in the two
years since he left the University until now
when he is gone from us. His humour of
being carried in a sedan chair, swathed in
blankets and reading a Latin poet, from his
rooms to the Turkish bath, is still remembered in his college.

When he came to live in town, he used
to quote 'Ambition was my idol, which was
broken'; but I think he never really

thought of it, certainly not in its common forms, but lived his artistic life naturally, as a bird sings. One or two ambitions he did, however, confide to his intimates. He desired to be regarded as a man to whom no chaste woman should be allowed to speak, an aim he would mention wistfully, in a manner inexpressibly touching, for he never achieved it. I did indeed persuade a friend of his and mine to cut him in the park one crowded afternoon; but his joy, which was as unrestrained as his proud nature permitted, was short-lived, for she was cruelly forgetful, and asked him to dinner the next day.

He confessed to me once that he regretted he had played ill his part in the drama of domestic life. It is true that no member of his family, except his mother, will allow you to mention his name now. There are a few women who look perplexed when

they hear it, and many who laugh. Some
men there are who disliked the smiling toler-
ance I have mentioned above; but those
who took advantage of his real humility to
swear at and romp with him—perhaps it
was a higher pride that made him allow
it—were fond of his society. People with
a common reputation of being artistic regarded him, I believe, with suspicion, since
his own devotion to art went far deeper
than theirs. Children bullied him, and he
was charming with old ladies.

The end was dramatic in its swiftness. A
little speech he made to a bishop who was
dining with his people was taken in ill
part by his father. He said it was the last
straw, and under cover of the metaphor sent
Tubby away from home, giving him but five
pounds a week on which to live his life.
The cruel injustice of his proceeding but
served to invigorate the spirits of my friend.

He made a noble effort to take the vulgar
burden of toil on to his shoulders. I pro-
cured him that beginning of a literary
career, a parcel of books to review. But
his devotion to art prevented his success.
He ranged the books on his table, forming
a charming harmony of colour, and spoke
of them wittily and well. His review was
merely a quotation from Shelley—

> ' I looked on them nine several days,
> And then I saw that they were bad.'

It was all his self-respect allowed him to
say ; but they sent him no more books. On
leaving home he went into a delightful
little flat in Jermyn Street, which the friend
whom he calls Bobby had just left, and
gave Thursday supper-parties, at which he
was an ideal host. But troubles came thick
upon him. His man refused to wear a dress
which Tubby had spent many hours in de-

signing. Nobody would print his poems. His expenditure exceeded his income.

Finally, he accepted his father's proposal he should go to Canada. It is supposed that the capital he has taken with him will serve him for at least six months, at the end of which we look to see him in our midst again.   G. S. S.

NOTE

What follows has been printed, with the exception of a few pages, in the 'National Observer,' as it was selected from time to time, and is reprinted by the kind permission of that journal.

ALAS!

A

I SHALL never forget the horror of the moment when I knew that Juliet loved me. Our intercourse had been so pleasant; it was hard that this barrier should be raised between us. Not, of course, that I realised its effect at once; I confess to a thrill of common humanity; I believe I even kissed her; I know I am only a man. But the rush of despondency was upon me soon : my mind, before my sense, had grasped the inevitable conclusion.

I had worshipped this woman. That subtle delight which (I dare to say) most strong natures feel in yielding them captive to a weaker had been mine for several months. I had gloried in fetching and carrying, and smiled at my contentment with her little words of thanks. As I turn the pages of my diary I find noted down all her rudenesses and rebuffs, and my musings—not cynical, but large-hearted—on the perversity of her sex. I had grown quite accustomed to her being unmarried, and was unreservedly happy. And now it was all over!

It was but last Thursday that, when I put my customary question, 'Can you not love me a little?' instead of her delightful 'I'm sorry, but I'm afraid I can't,' she hung her head and stammered, 'I don't know.' As I have confessed, I was gratified at first and went through the interview in an orthodox sort of way. It was as I sat in the smoking-room at my club—nobody seemed inclined to talk that night—that the ghastliness of the situation flashed upon me. If she had been married, one might have found a temporary solution; there would have been an experience, at least, in the sordid notoriety of the Divorce Court. (Ah, why did I abandon my caution, and venture off the track?) Even then, however, I knew that my nature could never

have supported a mutual passion for long.
To have my every movement followed by
loving eyes, to be adored, and to meet with
constant gratitude—it would have bored
me to death.   Still, I could have risked
that and gone through with the matter.
But an unmarried girl !   She would expect
a proposal of marriage.   Me, engaged to be
married !   Even in my misery I smiled at
the idea.   The inevitable suggestion of the
' young man ' and the ' Sunday out,' the
horrible stereotyped vulgarities, the foolish
engagement ring, the dreadful sense of being
imprisoned, the constant necessity of leaving charming strangers to talk to somebody
you know by heart (I thought of this view
impersonally, for I really loved Juliet)—the
utter impossibility of the whole business
simply confounded me, and I could not
allow myself to think of it.   I have never
affected a superiority over other men in the
common things of life, nor studied to seem
different from them, but this thing I could
not face ; it would make even me ridiculous.
To marry in secret and to go to some re-

mote place until the time for congratula-
tion was over was conceivable. . . . But I
knew she would not; no, no, some worthy,
common man was her proper mate; I was
not made for constancy. If I pained her
now, it was that she might escape a greater
pain when her love increased as mine
diminished. So I wrote a letter to Juliet,
I will copy down her answer, for it seems
an indication of a curiously frequent phase
in women. 'Dear Harry,' she wrote, ' you
are delightful! I hoped that Thursday
would lead to some agreeable variety in the
monotonous course of your foolishness, but
I never expected anything quite so delicious
as your letter. Of course I knew before it
arrived that your protestations meant nothing, or I should not have acted as I did.
Your idea of "sparing me future pain " is
most amusing, and I cannot be angry with
you. You can hardly think I need
apologise for humbugging you on Thursday; your vanity made it so absurdly easy.
If you would do some honest work, and
acquire an elementary sense of humour, you

would be quite a nice boy. You see I am very indulgently yours, J. C.'

Ah, the vanity of women, and the pains they are at to save it ! I fear she must have suffered keenly to deceive herself (or to try to deceive me) so grossly. Poor child, poor child !

THE OLD GENERATION

It seems worth the pains to make a note of my experience of to-day; for though it is trivial as regards my history, there is some instruction in this contact of a worthy, middle-aged pedagogue, with his curious narrowness of outlook and mediocre intelligence, and one like myself.

Even all those years ago, at school, I think that I differed from the others in seeing the excellent creature as he was. To some few he was of course the Doctor, a subject for abuse, but not for detailed criticism; to others he was a kindly superior or a great scholar; to me he was simply John Herbert Baxter, a poor human engine, striving with imperfect powers to do what an uninstructed habit of mind told him was his duty, a man of some reading doubtless, and a distinct ability for organisation, as impartial as his prejudices—those queer, unlovely prejudices !—allowed ; one who, Heaven help the poor fellow, had never lived.   As for his scholarship, such a stamp as University honours might put on a man was his, but even then I was more exigent in that matter and saw no trace in him of a comprehension of the Greek spirit; it is true I was never in the sixth, and so had no close observation of the result of his reading, but I often listened to his sermons in the chapel. I used to try to cultivate him in those days, and took an interest, a weary interest, perhaps, in his wife : poor dear, she was a sweet person in many ways.   When the rupture came, and his ridiculous, natural prejudices and absurd reverence for his silly rules inflicted an agreeable but undoubted injury upon me, and we parted, as I thought, for ever, my judgment of him was unaltered ; I felt as some Charles the First towards his executioner, and could find it in my heart to praise while I pitied him. So when we met

to-day there was no malice in my mind,
and I was ready to observe kindly this
specimen of a class that I have passed, as
it were, in the race of development.

I recognised him at once when he came
into my railway carriage (we were alone in
it), and I smiled at him as he sat down
opposite to me. As I expected, after greet-
ing me, his first question was: 'What are
you doing now?' To explain the folly of
it would have been to explain a philosophy
quite. unknown to him; so I merely waved
my hands, and inquired about his wife,
calling her dear lady, as indeed she was.
He answered stiffly, and I saw he remembered our ridiculous quarrel. But I wished
to have some profit from this encounter,
and even hoped he might go from it a
fresher and more clearly thinking man,
and therefore I tried, with gently search-
ing questions, to draw him out about his
work and its effects upon his mind. His
answers told me more than he (with that
bluff defensiveness which marks the national
character in the rough, and is so sad a com-

ment on our egotism) intended that they should, and the gulf between us seemed indeed impassable. I felt myself half angry at this imprisonment of an intellect I knew to be fairly capable, but also sorrowful— sorrowful almost to tears. At length our conversation came to this. He said to me: 'You spoke just now of "the elect." May I ask if you are one of them, and if so, who elected you and for what purpose?' I have a habit, when rude or sarcastic questions are addressed to me, of looking at the questioner with half-closed lids. It seemed to irritate the poor Doctor, and he asked me angrily if I were going to sleep. This gave me animation to speak plainly, and risking his affection for me I determined to throw a rope to this poor ignorant swimmer. 'I am elected,' I said smiling, 'to try to show you how inadequate are the ideas implied by your remarks; to restore to you what might have been. We have been talking for some time with a wall between us; I want you to scale it. I may seem to presume on too slight an acquaintance, but

from boyhood you have interested me.
Baxter,' I said, leaning forward and tap-
ping him on the knee, and speaking fami-
liarly, as to an equal, 'Baxter, do you never
feel that your life is wasted? It is wholly
spent in fulfilling a mechanical function
that hundreds of others would fulfil as
well as you. Doctrinal prejudices shut
you off from the joy of untrammelled
thinking, moral prejudices from the joy
of untrammelled living. Believe me both
sorts are foolish, and they are so dull.
You munch the dry bones of life; the
taste and the colour of it might not exist
for you. Be one of us; perform, if you
must, the vulgar duties of your calling,
but perform them with your mind set on
what is fine and rare. Rouse yourself. . . .'
Alas! He interrupted me. 'I suppose,'
he said, 'there are people who think this
sort of thing amusing, but I think it grossly
impertinent. But I won't resent it, as I
might. You used to be a fool, and now
you are a mass of conceit as well, and seem to
be fast losing your manners. Probably, what

little brains you have will go with them. It's a waste of words, but I may as well tell you, you are preparing for yourself a discontented manhood and a friendless old age.'

I put down his *ipsissima verba*, to be a standing warning to me that I never again try to fight against the perversity of his generation. It is all very sad and terribly disappointing. But the lesson is useful: we must live our lives and beware of altruism. I wished to be of service to this foolish brother, but after all I was not his keeper.

'BREATHE CLOSE UPON THE ASHES'

B

My host and I were left alone, and presently he went yawning to bed. I took a volume from the shelves at random, stretched my feet to the fire, and enjoyed the luxury of sorrowful retrospect. So we had met again. Romantic! A beautiful woman, certainly, but what things we read into them when a mere passing affection—like a cold or the gout—has possession of us. Yet I had not been deceived; she was very beautiful. But her gaiety and ease annoyed me; a wistful timidity of manner, and in place of her abundant health a worn and wasted appearance would have been more seemly. She must—I said to myself—be tired of her unlovely mediocrity by this time, because or though he seemed to treat her well. Once bit was twice shy, but I was not assured of it.

It was well for some things to be middle-aged, but, ah ! *le beau temps* . . . ! Then the door opened, and she came in most naturally, in a wondrous dark dressing-gown, the sleeves turned up with white silk : her hands were always perfect. The following is an exact account of this critical interview, as far as my memory serves me.

'I was with Nora in her room, and her husband said at the door he had left you alone. So I thought I would go and talk to you.'

She was perfectly calm, and I answered coldly : 'It is very good of you. Do you mind my smoking ?'

'Do I mind . . . I thought you might like to talk to me : we go away to-morrow. You did once, I think.'

The complacent smile in her untroubled face irritated me exceedingly. 'It is always charming to talk to you.'

'Harry, have you not forgiven me ?' Her confidence was purely outrageous. 'What,' I asked, 'do you think I have to forgive in you ?' 'Oh,' she replied, without the least sign of contrition; 'I think perhaps I was rather unkind to you. I did not know you were so much in earnest.'

'If,' I rejoined, and I felt my opening was clear—'If you wish me to tell you frankly what I think I have to forgive, it is that you made life a simple hell to me for weeks. Good God, how I suffered!'

'You are growing terribly stout, Harry.'

'No,' I said sternly, 'I can't laugh it off. I don't wish to talk about it. Let us change the subject.' 'Oh dear,' she said, and I felt it useless to strive against her levity; 'you are as bad as ever. Harry, I want to be friends.' She held out her hand. As I said, it was a very pretty hand, and I held it dubiously a moment. Then I shook it conventionally, and somehow it was I, and not she, who looked supremely ridiculous. She smiled more provokingly than ever.

'How is the world treating you, Harry?'

'All right, thank you.' I was quite unconcerned now. 'Have you been here long? I always think it the pleasantest house I know.'

'Only a week,' she replied, 'and we leave to-morrow.   My husband is never happy away from home.'

'Isn't he?' I said. 'I'm never happy anywhere!'

The childish sentimentality of it!   I nearly choked with anger at my folly. She was clearly gratified. She said softly, 'I wish I could help you to be happy; I would do almost anything to make you so.' She looked appealingly.   I felt the blood quick in me. I leaned forward and held one of her hands. 'Gwen, you can help me. You can make me very happy. If you knew how I loved you. . . . .' She laid the other hand on my head, very lightly. I felt I was trembling when I heard her voice. 'My poor boy, I will be an elder sister to you.'

I looked up: she was smiling with the air of an affable angel. I could have sworn at her. 'I don't want a sister.' She disengaged her hand. 'You tortured me once; you can make me amends a thousand times, if——' 'If what?' 'If you will accept, really accept my love, if . . . .' She had risen to her feet. 'It is very late; I must go to bed. Good-night.' She was gone with her last word.

I considered the alternatives. If her idea had been to amuse herself with the sight of a renewed but discreet passion, to keep me her lowly worshipper for ever, I was glad of the result. But if she had meant in good faith to make an advance to intimacy again, to atone for what was past, I feared I had been a little unamiable. This became a conviction, and I was eager to apologise. I spoke with her the next day for a minute apart as she went through the hall to dress for her departure. 'I have thought,' I said, 'about our conversation last night, and I wish to thank you.' 'Last night?' She looked straight at me. 'You forget I had gone to bed when you came into the drawing-room. Nora! Harry says he saw a vision or something in the library last night. You must make him write a story about it.' Did I hear her laugh as she went upstairs?

YOUNG ENGLAND

Sometimes I am concerned, thinking of my contemporaries—those, I mean, who are not of Us, and are yet from the accidents of life more or less my intimates. I mean those frank young barbarians who were some of my comrades at school and at Oxford, or from family or other ties familiar to me, whom I meet at my barbarian club (as I call it), or at dinners or country houses, who, knowing that I am young in mere years, and seeing that I take a part in their conversation, think me one of themselves. In truth, I find it restful to listen to their simple, homely talk, even to share their kindly, honest pleasures. I like to see their fresh young faces sparkle with merriment, as I suit some piece of simple irony to their comprehension. to watch their pathetic (is it not?) appreciation of their little successes in love and sport. Yet often, as I sit listening to their prattle, I feel wistful, thinking of what I have lost to gain my difference from them, wistful and almost regretful; I feel old, so old, sad, and very weary. I have eaten of the Tree of Knowledge, or rather of Thought, and lo! it is bitter in my mouth. But these are not the reflections I intended to make: I have chosen my part; *le jeu est fait* . . . I was saying I am sometimes concerned when I think of my contemporaries. It is not that I feel I neglect any duty of making them even as myself. The poor Doctor was warning of that futility: and moreover these young lives are better as they are. Should I cloud their unsophisticated happiness with questions they can never answer, with doubts they can never solve? Ah, no indeed. Not from heaven, as the poet feigned, came the precept 'Know thyself.' But I sometimes ask myself: Is it fair? I take their all, as it were, and give them so little of myself. They open themselves to me and keep

nothing back, while I show them but one
side, and an unimportant side, of my life
and character.   Now, as I would wish to be
remembered with kindness by my fellows, I
set down in this place my justification.   It
shows how I tried to be frank and to leave
no possibility of suspicion of deceit or reserve, and how it was proved to me that a
lower cannot grasp a higher mind, and is
in fact impatient of its existence, so that
one may fairly give his comrades only what
they are fitted to receive.   So far as my
memory serves me, I set down the incident
exactly as it occurred, even to the curious
and sometimes coarse dialect of my young
friend.

I was arranging my room after breakfast,
repairing the ungracious stiffness which is
always the beginning of the trials of my
day, when it struck me that my new rug
matched ill with my smoking suit.   The
better to test it I had sat down on the floor,
when the door was flung violently open,
and a needlessly loud voice proclaimed a
typical barbarian.   'Hullo, Tubby, as bad

as all that?' It was not the meaningless
nickname that distressed me: I permit it
for its obvious affection. But my nerves
are not what they were, and I felt helpless
as I watched him hang his hat on my little
Ganymede, and pull—so irrationally—the
chair I call my Lady's Chair from the spot
where long thought had placed it, and fill
the room with the smoke of his cigar: I had
denied myself a cigarette for my roses' sake.
He was a dear creature, but he was the
World, which had stormed my little fort of
individuality. My cat came purring to
comfort me, and I took courage to say what
was on my mind. 'Sit down, Frank,' I
said; 'I have something to say to you.'
'Look here, Tubby, I want you to come
racing.' Racing, racing! How dear and
how distant it all was! 'Ah, Frank,' I
said, 'when you have heard me you will
understand why I cannot go with you'—for
to the dust and the noise of a racecourse I
can no longer accommodate myself. 'Not
bad news, old man?' His sympathy
touched me; I rose and looked down at him

sadly. 'I fear it will be so to you.' Then
I thought I would prepare him, and going
to the table, took from the secret drawer
my Ballad of Shameful Kisses. 'Read it,' I
said simply. I watched his face, but his
class is trained to conceal emotion, and he
covered his with foolish jests. 'Poetry!' he
said. 'Tubby the Troubadour . . . O Lord!
. . . Thanks very much, old man; I'm not a
good judge, but it seems to rhyme all right.
Rather steep, though, isn't it? What you
might call indecent; what? But are you
coming racing?' 'I showed you my Ballad,'
I said slowly, 'that you may know what a
gulf there is between us.' 'You mean,' he
rejoined with his vacant laugh, 'that it's a
record of your experiences. I blush for you,
Tubby. I think you're a very wicked
young man. But will you come racing or
not?' 'Frank, I beg your pardon. You
see—do you not?—that our intercourse has
been one-sided. You have told me without
reserve all your life——' 'I'm damned if I
have,' the poor boy interrupted: but I con-
tinued pitilessly, 'And I, my dear child,

have lived a life apart, which you can never
enter. Art, my poor Frank . . .' Here he
broke in with a laugh, and threw a cushion
at me, and his horseplay finally stopped me.
'Shut up, Tubby. I give you ten minutes
to dress. As for art and all those sort of
things, if you take my advice you'd chuck
the whole boiling. It's all very well for
some chaps, but it's not in your line ; you
don't understand it, and people laugh at
you—I mean they will laugh at you, don't
you know? You don't look like it ; you do
yourself too well, and all that.'

Poor Frank ! I let him have his way and
we went racing together, and I soothed his
jealousy. I suppose he could not understand why I was so gentle with him that
day.

VARIUM ET MUTABILE

c

I count myself experienced in the ways of women, but I am yet at a loss to account for the changes that chanced at Bramleigh. It is, by the way, a pleasant house, where you are sure to find, in the midst of the stupid, idealess people who are everywhere, one or two poor spirits who have lived and can respond. It was there that, a week ago, I met Gwendoline yet again—did, in fact, take her in to dinner on the evening of my arrival. I took the liberty of an old friend to speak but little during the essential part of dinner, having little I cared to say to her while a need that, however dignified by art, is yet animal was in process of satisfaction. Then she rallied me, pretending to think my silence a question of preference for material things (an ancient joke against

me, at which I can afford to smile), and
we fell into the old manner. Neither
alluded to the past: we began, as it were,
a new game; but I saw she had not—as
how could she have?—forgotten. A talk
in the conservatory cemented, as I thought,
this basis of intimacy. But the next morning brought a change. She had promised
to walk with me to the Ruin, and I had
pondered much on my procedure. But
when she joined me in the hall, it was
to say—as though it were a matter of
course—'Charlie is coming; it's his first
visit, and he has never seen it.' Now I
can bear with their husbands, poor dears,
as a rule; but this creature is insufferable,
a rude person, a clown. I said rather
bitterly: 'I designed a comedy for two,
and you have made it a farce for three.'
She frowned and said: 'Would you like a
tragedy for one?' meaning, I suppose, that
she was afraid. An uncivilised touch in
her; but, it may be, some poor woman who
had known me . . . or her stupid husband
had shown jealousy. The walk was futile,

of course, and I confess my irritation prevented me from condescending to his level,
and even his piteous attempts at sarcasm
could not move me to relent. From that
time Gwendolen's manner became cold, distant, somewhat stupid, not elect. I supposed she was adopting an immemorial
device, and smiled at the incapacity for
change of tactics in her sex.

So I turned myself to a charming little
thing who was one of the party. She was
very pretty, and had little graceful move-
ments and little eager glances in her inno-
cent blue eyes. An appealing child! And
she could be taught, and took me for
teacher, and I found the office agreeable for
a week. There was a curious pleasure in
watching her wondering gaze, as I smiled
away her gods and illusions and showed her
a glimpse of what life might be.

And then came that atrocious cricket-
match. Bramleigh was to be matched with
some near place, and the men were con-
tinually making lists. I like to encourage
these things: to chat with a group while

the game is in progress, and cheer the
tedious affair with good-natured ridicule of
the players, and joke with them afterwards
about their feats and failures. This is, I
think, all that can be fairly expected of me,
and so when I was asked to play, of course
I laughingly declined. On the morning of
the game I was watching a merry little
group round Gwendolen, when presently she
came to me and begged me in her sweetest
manner to play as a favour to herself. The
very fact that she had been unamiable compelled me to acquiesce, for I had to avoid
any appearance of sulking (as of course she
knew), and thus oo women gain their ends.
'Dear lady,' I said, 'I can refuse you nothing.' But I was glad when I saw what
pleasure my complaisance gave these simple
folk. Doubtless, in some vague, dull way
they felt the difference between us, and
were proud that I should share their sport.
I heard them say : 'Tubby is going to play,'
and laugh in gleeful gratitude. . . . The
absurd mania for outdoor sports that afflicts
this country, and the ridiculous importance

attached to proficiency in them, make me a little sad. They were, no doubt, sorry that the accidents of the game repaid my kindness with continuous exertion and actual physical pain, and it was a charming thought that prompted them to laugh at me and say I had lost the match, by way of giving me the *rôle* of culprit—which is less annoying than his who forgives. I laughed with them, but I was weary, and sought my child early that evening for refreshment in her (I confess) pleasant admiration.

It was an odd experience. My little blue-eyed disciple would no more of my teaching; she turned our converse to that inane cricket-match, and made Bœotian jokes at my expense. She was utterly changed, no longer the admirer of a master, but the critic of an equal—nay, of an inferior!— that ignorant child of twenty. And yet nothing but a silly game had intervened. And Gwendolen came to me the next day, before I left, to make an odd little speech. 'Harry,' she said, 'I am penitent. I thought you had changed, and your conceit'—ah!

that old tribute to wisdom !—'seemed to have become genuine and not an affectation any more. One or two things you said to me seemed to imply . . . never mind ! And then you were so absurd and irritating with Charlie. I wanted him to like you, and I was very cross indeed. But I admired the good-natured way in which you made a fool of yourself yesterday, and you stood our chaff very well. Only, my dear boy, please don't . . . you understand ? '

Yes, I think I did. Divested of its odd artifices to conceal defeat, the little speech was plain, and my meeting with Gwendolen in the autumn will be interesting. She meant I was not to return her coldness, and I can afford a little magnanimity. But I am yet puzzled over the meaning of my blue-eyed child.

THE COMMON CURSE

To-NIGHT I have passed through a crisis, and though it was of a sordid and undignified kind, and one at which I can already laugh, it is fitting I should record it. Thinking to find the house empty when I came to sleep a night in it on my way through town, I came upon my father in the hall. He was in town on business, he told me, having left my mother and sisters in the country. I begged he would not allow my unexpected presence to keep him at home, for I intended to dine at the club. He asked me to dine with him *tête-à-tête* at home. I was surprised, for I had always believed him to be a little nervous in my society, although I was ever anxious to put him at his ease; I was also somewhat regretful, for in the present state of the house I could hardly expect

to eat there with that freedom from anxiety
and irritation which is all I require. But in
a way I was interested. I have never fallen
into the mistake of despising my father because he is old-fashioned and a little dull.
One's intellect is often tired and one craves
for a contrast, and the dear fellow's bluff,
downright manner and homely good sense
are often amusing and acceptable. Moreover, the savage virtues—courage and en-
durance — of which he has given proof
command an instinctive respect, and I like
to feel I must have them in my blood. In-
tellectually, also, *noblesse oblige*. But my
boyish dream of making him my companion
has long gone the way of all others. I tried
long and patiently, but the verdict of the
balance was irresistible. And long and
patiently I tried to be his companion, and
discussed—ah me, those discussions!—the
stupid, tedious questions of politics that
seemingly sufficed for his mental food, but
the wolf of originality would in spite of me
appear, as it were, under my sheep's clothing
of commonplaceness. No: good, worthy

man! The conviction was sorrowful but.
sure that he was better left to his politics
and newspapers and sport and friends—such
friends!—and I to my thoughts and my art.
Now and then I have observed him curiously, ready to welcome any development,
but save that increasing years render him
less and less tolerant of what he does not
understand, my father is almost Oriental in
his unchangeableness. To-night I was ready
for a fresh inspection.

Imperturbable as I believe my temper to
be, I could not trust myself to speak during
dinner. It is idle to deny that physical
causes shape our lives, and the thought of
how much of my better self must be warped
and wasted by that ghastly travesty of a
dinner, that criminal neglect of the most
elementary principles . . . who knows what
bitter trains of thought and evil impulses,
started to-night, may work unconsciously in
my brain and come back upon me to sour
my middle life? But when we were left
alone over our coffee I braced myself to talk
good-humouredly. 'It's a good opportu-

nity,' my excellent parent began, 'to talk
over something seriously with you.' 'Seri-
ousness always involves a risk,' I answered,
smiling, 'but if I can help you in any per-
plexity . . .' 'I want to know how long
this sort of thing's to go on.' I smiled
again at his simplicity. 'Dismissing a de-
pendant is an ungracious action,' I said,
'but surely not an impossible. I will sup-
port you, and I'm sure she cannot defend
this dinner.' 'Don't pretend to be a greater
fool than you are. How long do you pro-
pose to loaf about town? When am I to
hear of your earning some money?' The
utter unreason and irrelevancy of it silenced
me for a moment, and, in fact, having
generally deputed my mother (who can bear
with his absurd humours more easily than I)
to answer such questions, I was for a moment at a loss. He went on: 'Now, attend
to me, Harry.' The *ex cathedra* pose was
laughable, dear, honest man! 'Of course
this reading for the Bar is all humbug.
Some day you must earn your living. So
long as I live you can have a home here,

but if I die your mother won't be able to keep you.' His robust health is such a reproach to my poor overtaxed nerves that I could hardly feel his speech pathetic, and the coarseness of his phrases jarred painfully. I tried to turn the conversation into a general vein. 'Surely it is a mistake,' I said, 'to be haunted by these remote contingencies. Do you know, I rather wonder that a soldier like yourself is not free from it? Of course it is as true as it is obvious that we must all die, even so hale a man as you. "Death laughs,"' I murmured, half to myself—

'"Death laughs, breathing close and relentless
  In the nostrils and eyelids of lust"——'

'Never mind your poetry now,' he said, and I ended in a sigh. 'This is a question of business. You know I'm a plain, uncultivated person.' He is somewhat over-fond of parading his ignorance, but I was fain to re-assure him, and told him simply I respected him none the less on that account. My calmness seemed to irritate him, and I knew he would say more than he meant. I was never deficient in a sense of humour, and my amusement was fortunate, for his remark was outrageous : 'I intend that you shall go into a bank.'

The actual proposition was nothing, merely an idle expression of anger, though the hideous picture called up by my imagination was painful, and will, I fear, come back to me. But I felt that I must deal firmly with the situation, and prevent its recurrence. 'You will excuse me,' I said, 'if I do not follow you into details. I have no right to stultify myself with the mechanical drudgery you indicate, if it is necessary to notice that suggestion ; and, by the way, the law has long ceased to interest me. But you may be at ease. I have a gift which may be sold for silver and gold—the gift of song, father—though nothing but the needs of those dear to me would induce me to sell my child. Or if need be, I can live on a crust in an attic.' The good father had pursued some train of confused associations which prevented him from understanding me, for he said : 'If

you expect anything from your grandfather,
you may give that idea up. He says he
prefers a fit of the gout to listening to you.'
'It must be sad,' I said, 'to witness the
mental decay of a parent; I feel for you,
father. But I repeat; if need be, I can live
by my pen, live on bread and water in a
garret. So that is settled.' I glanced at
the clock. 'It's my belief, Harry,' he said,
with a recognisable flash of uncouth humour,
'that when you can't cadge any longer
you'll steal.' I thought it best to indulge
him with a laugh, and to end the interview,
having dealt manfully with the crisis, and
being in truth rather bored.

'Where are you going?' he asked. He
may have been sad that I did not stay with
him, but his absurdity to-night deserved a
mild recognition. 'To sup at the club,' I
answered. 'Go to the devil!' he said, the
dear, choleric old-world father! A sordid
crisis; but I am glad to have passed it.

'AGAINST STUPIDITY . . .'

I HAVE never shared that iconoclastic spirit of ridicule which some of my more thoughtful acquaintances show towards the Church. In truth, I take such a spirit to be an imperfection in their culture, a sign that taste is not equal to intellect, and I profess I would rather my own mind were as that of an ordinary bishop than that my culture should be merely intellectual. From a purely æsthetic point of view, there is much that is acceptable in the Church's ritual and surroundings. Why trouble about the import of her teachings ? I never listen to them, or merely smile when some fragment of quaint dogmatism breaks in on my repose. But I love to sit in some old cathedral and fancy myself a knight of the middle ages, ready to die—dear foolish fellow !—for his simple faith.

But this charm of mediævalism that I am
content should excuse the existence of an
institution which, as a thinker, I am forced
to pronounce an anachronism, is so rudely
broken by individual clergymen. I would
gladly listen if they talked to me of pale,
pure saints and quaint, ascetic martyrs, or
told me of beautiful, useless miracles which
they had read of in their curious lore. But,
to speak roughly, I find them painfully
modern. Their fare should be a manchet
of bread and a cup of spring water ; as it is
they join in our lunches and dinners. They
should know nothing of what has happened
for hundreds of years ; I find them interested in all the tedious subjects which
oppress me in the newspapers. Such an one
is Fairford, who is staying in this house. A
fine savage, beyond question, tall and broad :
he ' rowed stroke ' or did something of the
sort in my college boat at Oxford, and I
liked to count this young Hercules one of my
friends—so strong and noble as an animal,
and with all his sinews and muscles so utterly
my inferior. Intellectual, of course, the

good fellow could never be ; but what, from my point of view, absolutely unfits him for his calling is his full-blooded, hearty nature. I seek in a clergyman some faint echo of mediæval mystery and spirituality ; I think of that and then turn to this big, healthy creature talking of cricket and agriculture. The contrast is comical, but yet annoying ; and I made up my mind to try if I could not communicate to this honest Fairford some sense of the true fitness of things.

My opportunity came to-day when I found him smoking a pipe after luncheon in front of the house. A gentle stroll at this time is part of the wholesome discipline to which I subject myself, and I invited him to accompany me as far as the gate. 'Fairford,' I began, 'I want to talk to you on a subject that demands some apology. You will acquit me, I am sure, of any wish to be impertinent, if I say it is about yourself in connection with your profession.' My manner was designedly courtier-like ; he answered in his inappropriate English fashion : ' All right, fire away.' ' Well, then,' I said, ' my dear Fairford, conceive my shot to be the lightest of arrows; I only wish to suggest. I will not of course speak to you of your faith; that would be obtrusive and unnecessary; besides, in many ways your faith is charming.   It is in you, in the outward Fairford, that I would like to see some difference.   You have many excellent qualities, my good Fairford, but you are not mediæval.' 'Why should I be?' said my puzzled friend. (The obvious idea was quite new to him!)   'Because,' I said, and warmed to my task, 'because, my dear, good Fairford, you represent an institution whose charm and meaning are that it keeps the remote past with us.   In a sense you are past too; you are not modern as I am modern.   But in the ordinary sense you are very modern indeed.   What are your interests? you talk sport and politics for all the world like my father; you should be twenty generations earlier.   You laugh; you sing great noisy songs; you say you would shoot if you had time.   All that is wrong.   You should never speak above a murmur; I

think you should not be seen save in the
dimness of twilight.'

I knew of course he would not argue with
me, and desired merely to let my words sink
in. I was even prepared for some irrelevant
protestation. But I could not have ima-
gined the savage, animal outburst of un-
reasoning brute force with which he expressed
his impotent disagreement. Stopping suddenly, he said to me, 'Tubby, do you
wrestle?' I smiled and said, 'Nay, good
friend, I will wrestle with you in argument'·
when he, appearing not to hear my con-
cluding words, and throwing down his pipe,
sprang at me, grasped me with his great
bony arms, and flung me to the ground with
such violence that my straw hat fell off. I
was hurt physically; my breath came with
difficulty, and I feared the shock might have
injured my lungs; it was but a few minutes
after lunch. I looked up at him, and he,
great hulking savage, was laughing in
ignorant, stupid triumph. I was on the
point of addressing him with a sarcasm
which would have turned his triumph to

defeat, when I heard feminine laughter, and my hostess and Gwendolen came up. 'Harry,' said the latter, 'your beautiful tie is disarranged : what has happened ?' Fairford said : 'Tubby insisted on wrestling with the Church militant, and is out of training.' I remembered the attraction physical prowess has for all women, even, no doubt, for Gwendolen, and said with a laugh : 'We must wrestle again when I'm in practice, Fairford. For the present I yield to Christian muscularity.' I looked at Gwendolen with a little ironical smile, and she laughed again. After all, poor blundering Fairford's wild-beast-like resentment of enlightenment may not have been amiss.

LALAGE, THE BORE

I CANNOT call the heroine of last night by
the name I heard; it is inexpressibly painful
—like some flaunting jeweller's shop. That
which of right belongs to her is probably
far less odious, suggestive, it may be, of a
squalid and sordid life in some dismal,
monotonous slum—a life that to a spectator
from my own world might have some
whimsical charm of contrast and be the basis
of an odd romance. It might have recalled
Hazlitt to my memory, and his wayward
erotic fever. But the name I heard is
dreadful, dreadful in itself, and terribly
appropriate. I will call her Lalage. *Dulce
ridentem!* It was indeed a clear laugh,
coming across the thick buzz of conversation and the noise of knives and glasses,
which first induced me to regard her. Men

act from mingled motives; even I cannot always determine which it was that predominated in me. It was so last night. It was partly no doubt the warmth and gaiety of the little supper-party, which finished one of those boyish evenings I now and then permit myself; we had been merry and joyous, and I had bent to the humour of my companions more than is my wont. It was partly that laugh which seemed so pleasant then.

But there was another motive. I have never cared for the society of Lalage and her like. My reason is simple: they bore me to death. It is not that they are vulgar, or coarse, or mercenary. It is that from my point of view they are painfully, nay, shockingly respectable.

This may sound a paradox, but it is sadly true. Words are more than lives. Their lives are as they are; but they appear to keep intact the silly bourgeois prejudices in which they were bred. I say to them things which some women I know would argue about or smile at as the case might be;

those others cannot conceive that I am serious. They cannot understand that I do not share traditional interpretations of right and wrong; they insist tacitly on my regarding myself as a sinner and them as outcasts. Then again they are snobbish, reverencing accidental advantages of wealth and rank: some foolish companion richer than I—though quite uneducated—has frequently been preferred to me. So I avoid their society. But this avoidance has often been misunderstood by my friends, and attributed to a foolish morality at which I should be the first to blush. And last night they sported with my reluctance until I was grieved, and so I was introduced to Lalage.

Ah ! how unspeakably tedious she was ! I had hoped for a moment to find her a Faustine, or at least with something of Herodias' daughter. She was merely a respectable Cockney playing truant. I wanted her to be wild and wicked and abandoned, and she was nothing of the sort. I was inclined to be free and gay ; the vapid vulgarity with which she joked with Bobby,

who introduced us, sobered me at once. As
I took my seat in the little brougham I felt
I was going to execution. Her prettiness
was fast ebbing away. 'I like Bobby,' she
began; 'he's a great swell, isn't he?
Hasn't he a chance of being a duke?' I
saw her drift and answered decisively: 'I
trust not. Most dukes are middle-class,
and Bobby might be absorbed.' She stared,
and said: 'What a funny old thing you
are!' I looked out of the window. 'Give
me a cigarette,' she said next; 'I'm longing
to smoke. I didn't smoke in there; I don't
think ladies ought to in public, do you?'
I groaned, and she said: 'Cheer up, dear
boy.' 'Child,' I said, 'let us forget the
world and its conventions; let us be joyous
and free. Let us think we are Greeks of
old, before cold ascetics came to cloud the
lives of men. Let us——.' 'This *beastly*
cigarette ash has fallen on my cloak,' she
interrupted; 'brush it off!' I was silent
awhile, and then she called my attention to
the merits of the brougham and told me
how much she had to pay for it. I tried

desperately to enjoy the situation. I looked at Lalage ; decidedly she was pretty no longer. And then I shuddered when I remembered how the brand of champagne we had drunk was chosen against my advice. Yes ; I had indigestion. And then suddenly the thought of Gwendolen came to complete my discomfiture. It was utterly Philistine and commonplace that the thought of her should make me dislike my position ; I hated myself for it, but so it was. On a sudden impulse I stopped the brougham, explained that I was ill, and found means to appease Lalage's anger. For a moment as I strolled home I thought that perhaps my companions were right in a sense, and some idiotic principle I had learned in childhood had unconsciously restrained me. I felt guiltily moral and utterly dejected. Then I remembered that Rossetti had acted much as I had done, though perhaps our points of view were different.

A VICTORY OVER SELF

'My dear Harry, I was very angry when I read your letter. You must have been mad to write to me like that. It shows that you utterly failed to understand what I meant at Bramleigh, and it is just that—the sort of thing your letter is full of, I mean—which makes it impossible to keep up our old friendship. I am so very, very sorry, I liked you so much—we used to have such good fun together. These horrid new ideas of yours have quite spoiled you. Once and for all, Harry, I can't allow you to talk or write to me as you have been doing. How far it is real, and how far you think it clever or something, I don't know; in any case, I think it bad taste. Oh dear! Do be sensible,

Harry, and say you are sorry, and don't do it again, and please very much yours, Gwendolen. P.S.—You see, I can't forget your mother is like my elder sister. P.P.S. —Charlie saw your letter. I am sorry, because I know you did not mean anything, and he doesn't understand quite, and says he is going to speak to you about it. He is going to town to-day. You must not quarrel with him; you know he is rather quick-tempered.'

I think I read this curious document of femininity a dozen times. I copy it down, for it explains my forbearance with the absurd Charlie. It was the postscript which troubled me. I conceived the worthy man would have understood my letter to his wife as a bull understands a red rag. I have never thought it part of my *rôle* to dislike the intractable thing; it is not my fault that he is personally all that is bourgeois and hopeless. As for Gwendolen, I believe she was made to write that foolish letter, and I smiled as I saw how her desire to be appreciative struggled with the commands of her preposterous husband. For her sake I determined to control my temper, which I knew to be naturally sarcastic, if we should meet. But I thought it wiser to avoid a scene of silly recrimination altogether, and gave orders that I was not at home to him, and when I saw him coming towards me this morning in Piccadilly—he ought to have been killing things miles away!—I took a cab. All this trouble for a woman! But as I passed him with his inane, important swagger and his great red face, I was glad I had escaped the infliction of conversing with him.

But the stars in their courses fought against my benevolent intentions. When I went this afternoon to call on the only woman in London, he was in the room, and alone. After all, if I had to meet him it was well to do so thus; he could hardly make a very vulgar or violent display in the house of a woman who might come in at any moment. He looked so agricultural and uncomfortable that I rather pitied him, but could not deny myself the amusement of treating him

as a man of the world. 'Oh!' he said, 'I
wanted to see you. I happened to see
a letter you wrote to Gwendolen.' I sat
down and (I hope) regarded him com-
placently. 'Look here!' he went on in
his irritating, jerky manner, 'it may be
cursedly clever and all that, but I object
to it.' 'So strange,' I murmured. 'What?'
he said in his thick, dictatorial tones. 'So
strange,' I repeated, 'that you should object,
who are her husband. If you were a man
who was interested in her I could understand. But I forgot: I think you like
Gwendolen?' 'Like?' he asked, and gave
me one of his vacant, animal looks. 'Ah,'
I said, 'that is so refreshing of you! Most
of my married acquaintances loathe their
wives.' 'Be good enough to drop that
tone with me.' He drew himself up: 'Of
course you're only a boy,'—I smiled at his
method of retreat,—'and you're an old
friend of hers, and all that. But you've
annoyed her, and therefore annoyed me,
and without wishing to be ridiculous I
insist on your ceasing to do so.' He was

not without an element of rude dignity as
he said this, and I was pleased that he was
not violent.   I am always the slave of the
passing emotion, and said at once with
a sigh: 'You touch me, Charles; I will
spare her.'

I suppose it was the feeling that he had
been outdone in courtesy that angered him.
He made a step towards me frowning ludi-
crously.   We both heard a frou-frou on the
stairs, and I remarked that our interesting
conversation seemed to be at an end.   'Oh
no, it's not,' he said, 'we'll continue it
when we go.'   But I was determined to
stay him out, and not to give him an
opportunity to make himself more absurd
than he had already.   After a while I asked
leave to visit the schoolroom, and spent an
hour there, dissipating the foolish ideas and
superstitions I found the poor children had
imbibed from their governess.   When I
came down the agreeable Charles was gone.
There was a cab just outside the house and
I walked straight into it.   It was not too
soon; the creature had actually been walk-

ing about the square! Poor Gwendolen, to be tied to so dreadful a wretch as this! He swore vulgarly as I drove away. I was bored, but rather amused on the whole.

DISILLUSIONED

I HATE philanthropists. Chiefly, of course, as a question of principle. One's own associates arc monotonous, on the whole; they have an air of freedom from conventional restraint, but merely because it is the mode, and I often suspect the reality of their immorality. Even those few who arc the saving salt of society, and with whom the unloveliness of virtue is a matter of course, would, I fear, hang back if I put myself at their head for a career of flaunting, beautiful crime. I had one hope, which the philanthropists have taken away. I used to hope in the criminal class, in those who have taken no taint of respectability at their births. They are the patch of glorious red in the dull grey of our stupid civilisation—so absurd were it not so pitiful,—and

my blood boils when I hear of these un-
speakable philanthropists pulling down hot-
beds of vice and teaching helpless children
inane facts and antiquated ideas of pro-
perty.   In my own home I meet with little
sympathy.   My father is chairman of a
board or something, and investigates deserv-
ing cases.   My sister, too, is engaged to be
married to an embryo arch-fiend of philan-
thropy, and I am reminded that individually
and as a question of personal experience, I
think philanthropists impossible.   I have in
their society an uneasy feeling that they
find something wanting in me, such a feeling as many years ago I had in the society
of clergymen; one outgrows dogmas before
their indirect results, and thus I may not be
wholly regenerate in this matter.   Then if
you would not be thought guilty of a paradox, you have constantly to applaud the
lapse into virtue of some amusing sinner.
And they will suddenly demand money, or
ask you to share in some preposterous or
uncomfortable expedition.

But this creature who is engaged to be

married to my sister! I shall never forget
how, when I was a boy at Oxford, he per-
suaded my easy nature to conduct a party
of East-enders over the place, and give them
a meat-tea in my rooms. I had thought
they would get drunk and sing songs in the
quad, but I found them hopelessly respectable and most exasperatingly intelligent. I
had to explain my course of reading to
them, and when I tried to infuse a little
reason into their soulless and mission-ridden
existences they thought I was jesting, and
when I offered them brandy one of them
made me a speech. And the wretch who
had sent them wrote me a furious letter
when they returned. But for his philan-
thropy he would have been a tolerable
young man, as young men go. As it is, I
have heard him described as 'an earnest
fellow,' and as 'the ideal of a Christian
gentleman,' than which I can imagine nothing more pompous and tiresome and
ridiculous. He comes red-handed from his
settlement, or whatever it is called, and
bores us with accounts of the unfortunate

people he has snared into his nets, much as
Gwendolen's bucolic husband discusses his
bag when he has been out shooting.

One day he induced me to visit him
there, to take part in a sort of entertain-
ment. It meant dining in the middle of the
afternoon, but I went because I thought I
might meet members of the criminal class
not wholly converted. I was disgusted.
The people with whom I was made to play
chess reeked of virtue—a coarse expression
may be pardoned for a shock of disillusion,—
and one who looked more promising than
the others, and whom I asked to relate his
experiences as a burglar or a pickpocket,
complained that I had insulted him. It
ended in my being practically turned out,
and the next day my whole family harangued
me all through lunch.

I mention these things that my dis-
appointment of to-day may be the better
understood. I thought at last I was in
converse with unfettered criminals. He had
a big red scarf tied round his neck, a pecu-
liarity I had always associated with house-

breakers, and the woman with him was so
neat that I thought she must be a decoy.
The train was full, and the guard put them
into my carriage, apologising. I said I was
charmed, and at once began to talk with
them. The beginning was not easy, for he
seemed to resent being called 'my good
man,' which I had intended to put him at
his ease, and addressed me with a foolish
sarcasm as 'Yer rile 'ighness.' But they soon
thawed. I gave the man a cigar, and com-
plimented the woman's bonnet, and they were
all smiles. Then, being but a few minutes
from my destination, I plunged *in medias
res*, and pronounced a eulogy on a life of
crime. Perhaps they did not understand
me at first, for the man said it was 'like
being in church,' but all at once came a
catastrophe. Something I said, more par-
ticularly to the woman, angered them.
'Look 'ere, mister,' the man said (the dialect
does not amuse me, but I am told it does
others), 'you jest dry up. You may be a
dook, or as near as makes no bleedin' difference, but there ain't one of yer fine ladies

F

that's better than my old woman.' I had
no time to comment on the spurious sentimentality of his remark, and merely said
with a pleasant laugh: 'My worthy fellow,
they are not so good. They are mostly
tedious and respectable.' Then they stormed
at me, the woman inciting the man to
assault me. Explanation was wasted, but
the question was finally settled with what
he called 'the price of a pint.' We ex-
changed commonplaces awhile, and then I
became silent, and the man produced a
Philistine paper.

I suppose the criminal class does exist,
but I despair of meeting with it.

A FEMININE QUESTION

I HAVE acquired a very subtle understanding of woman, and the mistakes of my boyhood are quite impossible to me now. I can play upon her as upon an instrument of music, and smile as I touch the keys. But the smile is a little sad, for there was a romance in that strange, passionate discord I made once, which is gone. My case is the reverse of Byron's, who said he wished to love though he was no more beloved in turn: there are still young eyes that look wistfully on mine, but my love-making is over. 'No more on me the freshness of the heart can fall like dew'—how curious it all is! Did Nature keep pace with thought my hair would long ago have been grey.

Some such mournful reflections were running in my head this afternoon when Hughy

introduced me to his cousin. She seemed a
mirthful, frank young creature, and I know
how strong, often how sad, an attraction
there is for such gay, hopeful spirits in my
own world-weary melancholy. I thought I
too would be light and gay, and make no
sinister impression on her sunny existence.
It was an extraordinary experience. She
was quite different from other women, a
lusus naturae. There was none of that
charming inconsequence to which I am accustomed, especially in philosophical women.
She was literal and logical. I was so absolutely unprepared for it that possibly I
failed to show her how foolish a thing logic
is in the face of that deeper insight which
comes from life's experience.

She began by quoting some foolish question Hughy had just put to her, showing
the poor fellow's complete lack of all reading. 'Ah,' I said gaily, 'to be in the
Guards covers a multitude of ignorances:
Hughy looks sweet in his tunic. You must
not expect too much!' 'I expect,' she
answered, 'a great deal of you, because he

says you're very philosophical. I want so
much somebody to explain to me this theory
of ——.' She mentioned some horrid Ger-
man name which I had never heard. I do
not attempt to follow all the vagaries of
modern philosophy; there are so many
things to do in life, and mere book-learn-
ing is so futile. I do not at all value my
reputation for philosophy, which is surely
secure with those who can discriminate, but
I thought it a social duty to continue
the subject this pedantic girl had chosen.
'Which theory?' I asked her. She told
me; there was nothing charming in it, and
I have forgotten it now. 'It is not worth
explaining,' I said; 'what germ of truth
there is in it simply amounts to the only
practical outcome of all sound philosophy.'
'What is that?' she asked me, smiling for
some reason, thinking perhaps I would make
some silly joke, as Hughy would. 'It is,' I
said, folding my hands and speaking slowly,
' that you must live your life.'

There was never such a literal and persistent girl. She caught me up at once.

'Surely that is obvious: of course I must
live my life.' 'Obvious indeed,' I said sadly,
'but how difficult!' 'But what *do* you
mean? You might as well say I must dine
on my dinner.' A hopeless girl, but I tried
to make her see a minute particle of my
meaning. 'I mean you must be free and
joyous, not tyrannised over by foolish dogmas
of altruism, but fulfilling your own instincts
and desires.' 'Do just what I please? Be
thoroughly selfish? But that *wouldn't* be
my life. Why should you say that is
more my life than acting naturally, as one
is accustomed to act? One has certain in-
herited tendencies'—I smiled at the foolish
catchword—' and education forms them into
habits, and one's natural life is to act as
they direct.' 'Dear lady,' I said, desperately,
'don't let us quarrel about it. When you
have had my experience you will see what a
beautiful thing egotism is. Then you will
live your life; until then not.' 'What *do*
you——' she began, but broke off, and
asked, with a laugh, this utterly irrelevant
question: 'Do *you* wear a tunic too? And

do you look sweet in it?' How women care for these trifles !

A quite irrelevant question, but the only feminine thing she had said. I suppose she was posing; but she was an uncomfortable girl, and I do not want to meet her again.

BROUGHT BACK TO EARTH

How true it is that genius, to give the world of its sweetest, must be unhampered by sordid cares. Of late my muse has had no heart to sing. I came across a paper, tossed aside a while ago, which almost brought tears to my eyes. On the top I had written a title: 'A Dirge of Desire Dead,' and there followed a few lines which Sorrow herself seemed to have dictated to Song, and then—rows of squalid, hideous figures, and vulgar commercial symbols. Surely, I mused, here is all the pathos of life.

A care that had some romance or greatness in it—an unfaithful wife it might be, or a capricious mistress—I could have borne. Indeed, I have had my share of such sorrows, and those who have known the secret have wondered at my power of

seeming to enjoy dinners and the like with
a wolf gnawing my heart, as in the story of
the Spartan boy. It was the sordid, petty
nature of my troubles that destroyed my
peace and harassed my nerves. It made the
whole scheme of things, the whole frame-
work of society, seem so monstrous and
futile. Of mere debt, as such, I have
always made light. Nay, to be poor, as
the folly of the world condemns me to be—
who might have used riches so graciously—
to be poor and not to be in debt has seemed
mean-spirited; and I cannot remember a
time since my schooldays when I was what I
believe is called solvent. Debts sat lightly
and gracefully upon me, and I used to laugh
with my friends over imaginary trials. But
of late there seemed to have been a con-
spiracy to cause me absolute personal incon-
venience. I received threatening letters, in
which what chiefly annoyed me was the
obvious assumption that I should feel the
insults of the absurd writers; of course I
ignored them, but I am sure the effect on
me was depressing. A dreadful man was in

the habit of calling while I was at breakfast
and demanding money, and I had consider-
able difficulty in dismissing him from my
mind.   When I should have been meditat-
ing in quietude, I was forced to hold conversations with money-lenders, the very
furniture of whose rooms upset me for
the day, and of late even these labours
had been useless.   Perhaps the hardest,
because the most persistent wrong, was
that I was deprived of the simple enjoy-
ments of my fellows.   Life is hard to bear
very often, in any case, and that one should
lack the paltry distractions of town seemed
almost inconceivable.   I could not even go
to the silly things they call plays, and
because I owed money at places where we
dine and sup, I had often to eat my meals
—'meals' is the horribly appropriate word
—at home.   I had even to go to the man—
but why record these horrors?   It is morbid
to describe them fully; to indicate their
nature is enough.

It was only a week ago that Apollo freed
me, and as yet the nightmare of it all still

oppresses me. A sort of crisis had come, one man announcing his intention of writing to my father. My mother and my sister both refused to sell their jewels to help me; their barbaric preference of stones (for they know nothing of their beautiful symbolism) to my peace of mind wounded me, but I am a man of strong natural affection, and I have forgiven them before they have asked forgiveness. Then I went to my father with my rows of figures. On the whole, the scene was artistic. I am naturally dramatic, and like to play the parts of life with zest. The repentant prodigal is a foolish and contemptible person, but I felt I owed it to my father to act it vigorously. My father's rage was all that the most exacting critic could have demanded. It was a pleasant little comedy, and not until quite the end of it did I drop unthinkingly into my natural manner and smile at my father's solemnity about the 'last time.' I felt disproportionately grateful to him for removing my cares, for it cost him but little thought or pains, and I agreed readily to

conform to the wish which haunts him that
I should 'do some work.'   How far a sort
of half promise made in such a trite little
domestic play can bind one in real life, I am
not casuist enough to determine.   In the
true sense of the word there is more 'work'
in a ballad of mine than in years of his
soldiering.   But work in his sense would
be an experience which I am seriously inclined to invite.

FRONTIS NULLA FIDES

I HAVE long passed that stage of intellectual development in which we fret at middle-class conventions. I contemplate them now with infinite delight in their absurdities. By 'middle-class' I do not, of course, mean to imply any ridiculous social distinction : my own father, excellent person that he is, is quite middle-class in his attitude towards life, and the boyish zeal which used to prompt me to make a proselyte of him is gone—alas ! —with the snows of yesteryear. On the other hand, I conversed but last week with a person in the street, a quite uneducated person without ideals, who seemed free from commonplace restrictions. By middle-class conventions I mean chiefly respect for so-called virtues—truth, for instance, which is simply want of imagination, or prudence in

money matters, which is simply grovelling
cowardice—and that curious reticence about
things which may be made charming in conversation. I no longer fret at these follies,
but try to amuse myself with them, and have
often beguiled the weariness of a dinner at
home by leading my father to the verge of
some forbidden topic and observing his confusion. I even congratulated my aunt with
a perfectly grave and sympathetic face on
her 'silver marriage,' as though twenty-five
years of tedious constancy were a credit to
her. It was therefore doubly hard on me
that an alleged want of respect for 'propriety'
—I really think they are quite capable of
using the word—should be made the excuse
for one of those vulgar domestic brawls
which my nerves have been latterly unable
to bear.

I was deceived in a little woman who
came to stay with us the other day. Of
course you can never be quite sure what
things will please a woman in conversation.
Things which I think disgusting they do not
mind—I have heard one discuss the food

provided in some workhouse,—while they will look scandalised at little quaint romances, little harmless vagaries of passion. But this one was so prettily arch and talked so gaily that I took her for an artistic, unprejudiced person, for one of ourselves. She came into the smoking-room in the afternoon and smoked a cigarette with me. We talked unaffectedly, and laughed at the follies of some vicar's wife she told me about, and I thought she would be amused with a story of something which happened to Hughy in Paris, the pink silk story. There is a strain of odd humorous pathos in it, and I told it as a little idyll of a city, as it is, with no idea that she would see anything in it that any modern person would dislike. Before I had arrived at the end she rose, said something about 'going too far,' and left me. Of course I supposed she was in fun, and admired the art with which she managed to blush. I resumed a diverting book about the early Fathers, and forgot her.

In half an hour a storm was upon me. It seems the deceptive little thing had suggested to my mother that I ought to be cautioned for my own sake not to tell such 'improper stories,' and that my father had overheard her. He came into the smoking-room simply foaming, and most ridiculous. 'Are you drunk, sir?' he shouted. 'Dear father,' I replied with dignity, 'I am never drunk with wine, nor at present am I drunk with love. One may be drunk with life, but alas!——' 'What the devil do you mean by insulting a lady under my roof?' I love his melodramatic expressions, but when he talks about his roof it is always the prelude to a tedious harangue. In this instance I endured it meekly, since I could only defend myself at the expense (in his eyes) of our guest. But I happened to be alone with her in the drawing-room before dinner, and could not forbear to turn a Philistine weapon against herself. 'I am so sorry,' I said con-tritely, 'that I annoyed you this afternoon. But you know you must have misunderstood my little idyll. I must have told it badly; it is really quite free from anything horrid.' She looked a little confused, and I smiled inwardly.

THE CLOSING SCENE

THIS day I leave my native land. It is five in the morning, the last of the companions who spent the evening with me is gone, and I sit in my lonely room to end this account of my life so far before sleeping a few hours. When they dine to-night I shall be far away. It is intensely dramatic. A weaker man might well shed tears, but my eyes are dry. I look round the room and observe the artistic confusion in the soft light of the lamps—my fur coat lying carelessly on the sofa, my gloves thrown on the floor. I look at myself in the glass, and see a white shirt and tie—symbols of civilisation, such as it is, perhaps worn for the last time—the soft dreamy satin of my smoking-coat, and above a face, white indeed, but resolute.

I suppose my friends meant to be sympathetic to-night, but sometimes their tone jarred on me a little. Themselves children of luxury, they can hardly realise what it is to thread impenetrable forests and fight with the naked forces of nature. Hughy, indeed, in the little speech he made at supper, spoke of me lassoing wild horses and duelling across a handkerchief with desperadoes, and his voice for a moment trembled; but the others laughed. Perhaps they think I am insincere and that I shall avoid doing these things. How little they know me! We dined together and went to the barbarous, plush place I am so weary of, and had supper in a private room. I talked gaily and naturally, and played my part of devil-may-care indifference. All perhaps for the last time! Well, I am tired of it: let it go. I suppose it is of no use to take my evening clothes to Canada.

The changes of the last few weeks rise clearly in my head, as they say happens to drowning men. I see myself, because of his wretched intolerance, leaving my father's house. Then these rooms which needed so

much thought after Bobby's crude tastes
to make them seemly, and the sickening
obstinacy of the man, who refused to
harmonise himself with my plan of colour.
I was determined to earn my bread, and
speedily found how hopeless the idea was,
unless I would abandon my better self.
And then the discovery of the miserable
inadequacy of the pittance my father gave
me to the needs of life, and the crueller
discovery of the dark side of human nature,
when I went to him and to my other relations
for aid. I have never thought very highly
of my fellow-creatures—they are far less
graceful than cats—but I had given them
credit for a few ordinary virtues. My experience when I needed a little paltry money
robbed me of my faith in man, and
Gwendolen has taken from me my faith
in woman. I had forgiven her the reticence
and subterfuges which her intolerable
husband made necessary, but that she
should fail me when the crisis came and
refuse to go with me to a freer life across
the seas pained me bitterly. Perhaps,

though, she was right artistically : the idea was rather conventional and trite.   But morally she was utterly disappointing.

In my last interview with my father, in which he utterly failed to rise to the situation, he said that I had wasted my life, and curiously enough the thought has recurred to me, though of course from a point of view very different from his.   It may be that my life has been warped by the conventions of my country.   I have merely humoured them good-naturedly from the principle of *noblesse oblige*, but they may have unconsciously hampered my inner life. Yes, my nature will expand in this wild land.   Of course I have avoided, so far as I could, learning anything about it, that my impressions might be absolutely free.   My father spoke of an agent whom I was to see on my arrival : I think he wants me to go into a bank out there.   But I shall make straight for the forests, or the mountains, or whatever they are, and try to forget.   I believe people shoot one another there : I have never killed a man, and it may be an experience—the lust for slaughter. They dress picturesquely : probably a red sash will be the keynote of my scheme.

But I must bring these thoughts to a conclusion. A page in my life is turned for ever. I have tried to compromise between the imperfect civilisation I found and my own nature, and the compromise has failed. My relations of course—when did they ever appreciate such an one as I ? I went among the abandoned, the outcasts of society, and found them as tame and conventional as those I had left, only less polite. I loved a woman, and she allowed all sorts of anachronistic fantasies to stand between us. Even my friends, even Bobby and Hughy and the others, failed to stand shoulder to shoulder with me in my sordid difficulties, although they knew I had no bourgeois prejudices on the subject. It is well : I will go from them all, and perhaps among savage Indians may find peace. And perhaps when some of those I have left read what I have written, and see what they have lost, they will weep for what might have been.

Printed by T. and A. CONSTABLE, Printers to Her Majesty
at the Edinburgh University Press

www.ingramcontent.com/pod-product-compliance
Lightning Source LLC
Chambersburg PA
CBHW031928060726
47496CB00008BA/2428